MY WHEELCHAIR IS A REALCHAIR

IS A REALCHAIR

Written and Photographed by Maida Jane Sperling

Photographic illustrations Copyright © 1996
by Maida Jane Sperling. 15749-SPER
Library of Congress Number: 2002092987
ISBN #:   Softcover   1-4010-6505-8

Book Designer: Rick Contreras
Art Director: Mike Nardone

To order additional copies of this book, contact:
Xlibris Corporation
1-888-795-4274
www.Xlibris.com
Orders@Xlibris.com

My WHEELCHAIR is a REALCHAIR

written and photographed by
Maida Sperling

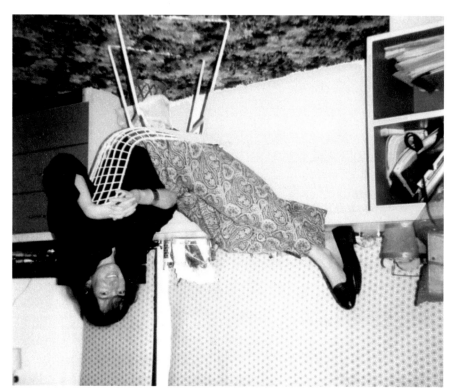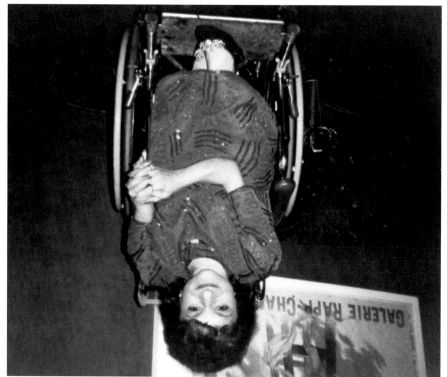

For
Amy and Valerie,
in all their chairs,
and
Gery, who chair'd me on
and
in memory of
Dr. Harold Sofield,
an orthopedic innovator of marvelous humor,
intellect, compassion and generosity,
without whom many ongoing stories would never have had a happy ending.

WHEELCHAIR REALCHAIR

My wheelchair is a realchair
But when I'm in it, people stare.
They speak to my Mom
Like I'm not even there!
That makes me feel invisible -
It's awfully unfair.
It's as if I couldn't hear them,
Or wouldn't give a care.
They ask my Mom rude questions
While they pat me on my hair.
It's plain as can be
That they see my chair.
But talk to me?
Well, they just don't dare.
I wish they'd ask me
HOW? WHY? WHEN? WHERE?
First I'd say, "Hi,
I'm Sheila Claire.
There are so many things
I'd love to share!"

Now if you should see me wheeling
I know you'll be aware
You can ask, I can answer,
We can talk and compare,
While you walk at my side
And I ride
In my real wheelchair.

If you should go to move my chair,
Before you take me anywhere,
I wish you'd ask me, "Are you ready?"
And give me time to get real steady,
Or give me a chance to finish talking
Before you start abruptly walking,
Please let me say when to stay or go,
And please do listen if I ask you to slow.

Here are some things
I like to do
With my wheelchair
And a friend or two...

DRESSING UP

Kim is the name
Of my very best friend.
We love to dress up
So we can pretend.
It doesn't matter
One little bit
If the things we put on
Don't really fit.
Mom gives us hats
Or sister's old shoes -
There's no piece of clothing
That we can't use.
We help each other
To tuck things in
Or hold them together
With a safety pin.
We'll try them on
If they're old or new,
Then we'll look in the mirror
And admire our view,
And we'll make up a story
That we wish would come true.

GARDENING

We made a garden
In Ben's backyard.
In the beginning
We worked very hard.
Now we hurry to tend it
When school is done
Cause this kind of work
Is really fun!
Rob and Ben
Used a shovel and rake
To smooth the earth
So we could shake
Seeds for flowers
In row after row.
My job is to water them -
That helps them grow.

VISITING ROB'S HOUSE

When Rob asks me
To come over and play,
Our Moms sure have
A lot to say,
Cause now <u>they're</u> friends
And here's what's new:
Sometimes they go places
Without us two!

AND PLAYING PIANO

I play in the orchestra
That we have at school,
And I take piano lessons -
That's really cool.
Rob and I learned
To play a duet.
He's in our school band
Where he plays the drum set.
Rob's Mom's a singer,
Her voice is so sweet.
We help her to practice,
She shows us the beat.
It's like a real concert
And she's ever so kind -
If we hit a wrong note,
She says, "Never you mind!"

MAKING LUNCH

When I'm in the kitchen,
I'm always aware
That the stove should be used
With a great deal of care.
My Mom and Dad
Have helped me learn
How to cook on the burners
But avoid a burn.

There's plenty of time
Cause it's Saturday,
So Kim came over
To eat, then play.
My Dad was home,
So we cooked for three.
He said his burger
Was as good as it could be!
When it comes to cooking,
I'm more than able,

And my wheelchair fits
At most any table.
First we set places
Then we carry a plate.
I can use my lap
And it works out great.
We do the clearing,
We wash and dry,
We sponge the counters
(well, at least we try),
We wrap the leftovers
And put them away,
Then off to my room
For an afternoon's play.

SCHOOL

I come to school with my friends
In a group.
Where we cross the street
You can see that a scoop
Has been taken out
Of the corner curb.
Look for it in your city
Or in your suburb.
That shape's called a <u>cutout:</u>
It's a low incline
From the gutter to the pavement
In a straight, smooth line
And with my wheelchair,
It's a cinch to climb.

My classroom holds
Such wonderful things.
When I come through the door
Each day it brings
Me books that tell me
What I'm curious about,
Pets to care for,
Plants to sprout,

Numbers and letters -
Teacher makes them a game -
Songs, stories, projects,
That are never the same.
We put on plays,
We get to rest,
We paint pictures at our easels
And I love that best.
We decorate the room
Or make a holiday card,
We eat lunch and snacks
And we play in the yard.

School in my wheelchair
With all my friends -
Each and every day
I'm sad when it ends.

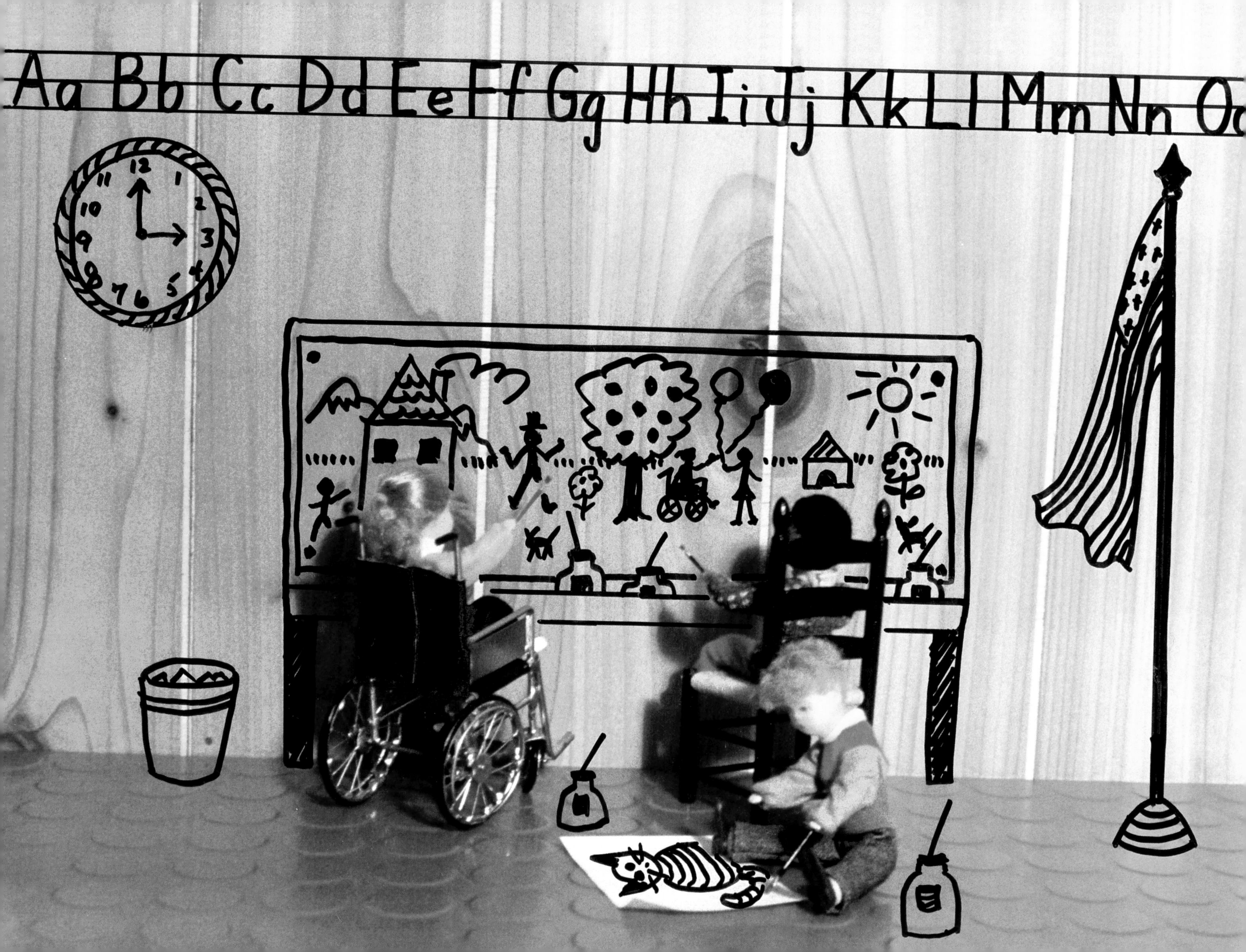
Aa Bb Cc Dd Ee Ff Gg Hh Ii Jj Kk Ll Mm Nn

AT PICNICS AND IN OTHER PLACES

I go on picnics
And I fly kites,
And my wheelchair takes me
Up to the heights.
At the movies or library
I bring my own chair,
Even to the ball game
Or the circus or a fair.
So I feel right at home
Just about anywhere -
Though you won't <u>always</u> find me
Seated in my chair.

I wheel right up
To my bed or a sofa.
If the height is right
I know I can go for
A trip from my chair
To another place:

I call this "transferring"
To a new base.
My arms are strong,
They help me across.
But some people in wheelchairs
Don't have enough force,
So they ask a helper
To give them a lift
When there's somewhere
They'd like to shift.
In my tub and shower
There's a special seat:
I take care of myself
And that feels neat!
We found that seat
In a wonderful store.
For people in wheelchairs,
It has gadgets galore.

IN MY LIVING ROOM WITH MY BOOKS

The shop sells a basket
For the back of my chair -
I put my school books
And my lunch box there.
They've a long-handled grabber
That's made of wood.
Kind of looks like a scissors
And its grip is good.
It helps me reach
What's high overhead
Or pick up what's dropped
On the floor instead.

Now you've learned a great deal
About wheelchairs and me.
Did it change how you feel?
And do you agree?
That WHEELCHAIRS are REALCHAIRS
Wherever they go,
And the people in them
Would be nice to know.

What can you think of
That's fun for two
That you and <u>your</u>
Wheelchair friend can do?
Here are some pages
Where you can draw
What you and your friend
Get together for.

With my thanks to:

Sharon Margulis, whose down-sized world is called
        The Magic of Miniatures, for successfully
        locating the populace and furnishings on my Lilliput list.

Erna Meyer, miniaturist doll creator, whose small
        folk were capable of bending to my every
        photographic requirement; and for finding the
        time to custom fashion a character for special
        appearance here.

Susan Stassa, early childhood specialist,
        in the Children's Room of the
        White Plains Library, for insights,
        expertise, and for her incomparable presence.

Joellyn and Burt Goodman, for helpfully mapping
        the field and following my progress through
        it with interest and encouragement; and for
        the generosities of their friendship.

Maida Sperling has worked as a photographer, cartoonist and jewelry designer. This is her first book. She hopes that WHEELCHAIR REALCHAIR will help remove some of the uncertainties that people feel when meeting someone who is wheelchair seated.

To e-mail Maida Sperling,
send to:
imager@iopener.net

To order additional copies of this book, contact:
Xlibris Corporation
1-888-795-4274
www.Xlibris.com
Orders@Xlibris.com